671.3   Boraas
Bor
        Machinist

DATE DUE

CAREER EXPLORATION

Machinist

by Tracey Boraas

Consultant:
Charles Arnold
Minnesota Precision Manufacturing Association
and
Thomas Nielsen, Machinist
Waterous, Co.

CAPSTONE BOOKS
an imprint of Capstone Press
Mankato, Minnesota

Capstone Books are published by Capstone Press
151 Good Counsel Drive, P.O. Box 669, Mankato, Minnesota 56002
http://www.capstone-press.com

Library of Congress Cataloging-in-Publication Data
Boraas, Tracey
     Machinist/by Tracey Boraas.
     p. cm.—(Career exploration)
     Includes bibliographical references and index.
     Summary: Describes the career of machinist including educational
requirements, duties, workplace, salary, employment outlook, and possible
future positions.
     ISBN 0-7368-0491-9
     1. Machinists—Vocational guidance—Juvenile literature. [1. Machinists—
Vocational guidance. 2. Vocational guidance.] I. Title. II. Series.
TJ1167.B57 2000
671.3'5'023—dc21   99-054148

Editorial Credits
Connie R. Colwell, editor; Steve Christensen, cover designer; Kia Bielke, production
     designer and illustrator; Heidi Schoof, photo researcher

Photo Credits
MPMA, 10, 19, 22, 46; MPMA/Roberts Automatic, cover 6, 13; Gauthier
     Industries, 9; ProtoTEK, 31, 38
Photo Network, 16; Dennis Mac Donald, 28; Mark Sherman, 35; David Peevers, 41
Photri Microstock/Skjold, 26
Unicorn Stock Photos/Steve Bourgeois, 14
Uniphoto/Jim Schafer, 20
Visuals Unlimited/Jeff Greenberg, 36

1 2 3 4 5 6 05 04 03 02 01 00

Table of Contents

Fast Facts

Career Title	Machinist
O*NET Number	89108
DOT Cluster (Dictionary of Occupational Titles)	Machine trades occupations
DOT Number	600.280-022
GOE Number (Guide for Occupational Exploration)	05.05.07
NOC Number (National Occupational Classification-Canada)	723
Salary Range (U.S. Bureau of Labor Statistics and Human Resources Development Canada, late 1990s figures)	U.S.: $16,120 to $55,000 Canada: $20,500 to $54,800 (Canadian dollars)
Minimum Educational Requirements	U.S.: none Canada: none
Certification/Licensing Requirements	U.S.: none Canada: none

Subject Knowledge	Mathematics; physics; blueprint reading; metal working; drafting; basic computers; basic electronics
Personal Abilities/Skills	Skillfully use hand tools or machines; read blueprints and drawings of items to be made; measure, cut, or work on materials or objects with great precision; picture what the finished product will look like
Job Outlook	U.S.: good Canada: good
Personal Interests	Mechanical: interest in applying mechanical principles to practical situations, using machines, hand tools, or techniques
Similar Types of Jobs	Tool and die maker; metalworking and plastics-working machine operator; tool planner; and instrument maker

Chapter 1

Machinist

Machinists work in precision manufacturing. This involves shaping materials such as iron, steel, bronze, aluminum, and plastic into various parts. These parts can be thousands of different shapes and sizes. The parts may be used to make products such as motorcycles, ballpoint pens, or automobiles. Some machinists build the machines that workers use to make products. Machinists may even make the tools and machines that other machinists use in their jobs.

Duties

Machinists plan the steps needed to make each part. They determine the exact size each product must be. They determine how strong or flexible each product should be. Flexible parts bend easily.

Machinists shape materials such as iron, steel, bronze, aluminum, and plastic into various parts.

Machinists also select the materials needed to make each product.

Machinists use machines to make product parts. Machinists must set up the machines they need for each job. They must adjust machine controls. Machinists then watch the machines to make sure they are working correctly. They adjust the machines when necessary.

Machinists check the finished parts. These parts may be a single product such as a nut or bolt. The products also may be one of several manufactured parts. These parts will fit together to make one larger product such as a motorcycle.

Machinists at Work

Machinists work in a variety of settings. Some work in small machining shops. Other machinists work for large manufacturing companies. These companies have their own machining departments.

Machinists' duties depend on where they work. Some machinists work for companies that make business or factory machines. Other machinists work for companies that make aircraft or motor vehicle parts. Some machinists

Machinists make a variety of parts.

do not make products. They maintain and repair business and factory machines.

Programmers are machinists who direct machinery to operate without human control. Programmers use a keyboard to program commands into a computer numerical control (CNC) machine. This process allows other machines to operate automatically. Programmers usually work in offices that are separate from machine shops.

Tools and Machines
Machinists use many types of tools and machines

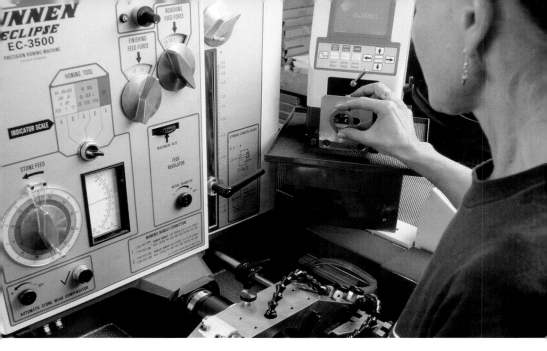

Machinists can measure very small distances.

in their jobs. They use machining tools to shape parts. Machinists use three main types of machining tools. They use grinding machines that shape parts by grinding them. They use turning machines such as lathes. Machinists turn parts against these cutting tools to shape the parts. Machinists also use milling machines. These machines hold parts steady while cutting devices move across and shape them.

Machinists often use machines. Machinists program commands into CNC machines using a keyboard. The CNC machine then directs other machines such as lathes to make parts. Machinists do not need to operate the machines. The CNC machine can make as many copies of the part as needed.

Machinists also use measuring tools. Machinists use micrometers to measure very small distances. Machinists can measure distances as small as .0001 inch (.00003 centimeter) by using a micrometer. Machinists use height gauges to measure the height of a part. They use gauge blocks to measure the size of slots or holes in certain parts. Each finished part must meet exact size, shape, and weight standards.

What Machinists Need to Know

Machinists should be skilled at using machines and tools. They must be able to operate different types of tools. They should know which types of machines and tools are needed to make particular parts.

Machinists should have other skills. Math skills help machinists measure parts. Machinists should know how to read blueprints. These detailed plans show how to make a part or product. Skills in blueprint reading help machinists follow guides when making parts. Drafting skills help machinists draw blueprints.

Machinists should have a basic knowledge of electronics and computers. Electronics skills help machinists set up and operate machines. Today, computers control many machines. Machinists must be able to operate these computers and instruct them to create parts.

Specialists

Machinists may specialize in a particular job. Toolmakers make tools such as jigs and gauges. Jigs hold parts in place while machinists work on them. Gauges are instruments used for measurement. Die makers make tools used to punch out and form metal products. These products include the clips on ballpoint pens. Mold makers specialize in building tools that shape liquid materials such as plastic into solid products.

Machinists must know how to use a variety of tools.

Instrument makers work with inventors and scientists. Instrument makers develop models of the inventors' and scientists' ideas and designs. They make models of products such as medical clamps. These instruments hold skin or tissue while doctors perform surgery. Instrument makers work from sketches, drawings, or spoken instructions. They may need to correct or change the models many times before the instruments are finished.

Chapter 2

Day-to-Day Activities

Machinists' duties vary each day. Machinists may spend five days on one complicated part. Or they may produce 200 simple parts in one hour.

Machinists' daily procedures depend on their employers' needs. Each shop and company has different needs. These depend on the number of machinists the shop or company employs. A shop with only two machinists may need them to perform various duties. A company with many machinists may allow them to specialize in one type of work. Companies' needs also depend on the products they produce.

Machinists' duties vary each day.

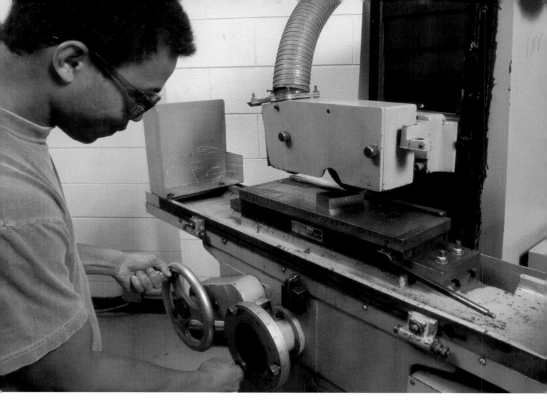

Machinists decide which machines and tools they need to complete a project.

Assigned Projects

Machinists usually begin a project by receiving an assignment from a supervisor. Supervisors sometimes give these assignments in writing. Machinists also may read blueprints to determine their assignments.

Machinists then plan the steps needed to complete the assigned job. They study blueprints, sketches, drawings, and manuals. Manuals contain detailed information about particular types of machines. Machinists sometimes study sample parts. These parts give machinists ideas about how to construct the assigned parts.

Machinists next decide which machines and tools they need to complete the projects. They fasten the tools onto the machines. Machinists must select tools for each project carefully. Each tool cuts and shapes in a slightly different manner.

Machinists also select the materials needed for the job. Some parts should be made of plastic. Other parts may need to be made of metal. Machinists must know the qualities of many types of materials. This helps them select the proper materials for each job.

Performing the Job

Most machinists use CNC machines to perform their jobs. Machinists' commands tell the machines how deep and at what angles the materials must be cut. Machinists set the CNC machine controls. The controls adjust how fast the materials feed through the machine. The

CNC machine then can direct other machines to cut and shape the materials.

Some shops or companies hire computer programmers to write programs for their CNC machines. Machinists can use these programs to perform their jobs. Machinists then do not need to program the CNC machines themselves.

Machinists start the machines after entering the programming commands. The machines then begin cutting and shaping the materials. Most machinists know how to operate all machines in the shop or center. Machinists observe the machines while they are operating. They adjust the machines' controls or programs as needed until the part is finished.

Machinists examine the finished parts. Machinists may need to deburr parts. They clean the parts and file the parts' rough edges. Machinists then use measuring instruments to determine if the product meets the exact size requirements.

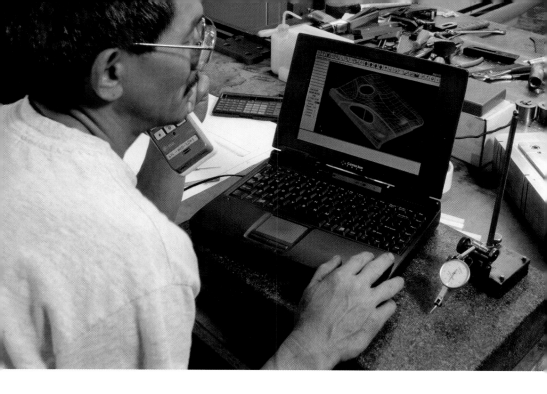

Some shops or companies hire computer programmers to write programs for their CNC machines.

Machinists sometimes fit certain machined parts together to form a larger product. Machinists may use jigs, power tools, or hand tools to put these parts together. They may harden, grind, or file parts before the job is completed.

Chapter 3

The Right Candidate

Machinists' job duties may vary. But machinists should share some basic abilities and interests.

Abilities and Interests

Machinists should be skilled at operating various machines and tools. They also should know how to set up the equipment in their shops or companies.

Machinists must be able to work without direct supervision. They must be able to complete jobs on their own. Machinists also must complete tasks on time.

Machinists must have good vision and hand-eye coordination. These abilities help machinists perform detailed tasks with their

Machinists should be skilled at operating various machines and tools.

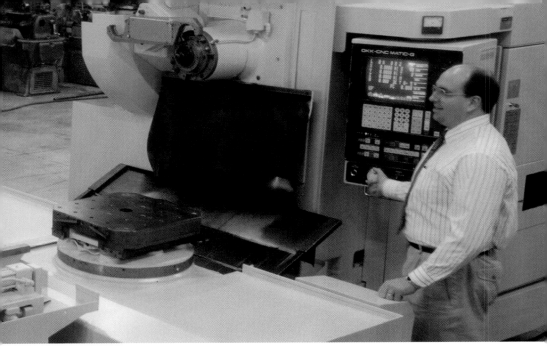

Today, computers control many machines.

eyes, hands, and fingers. Some parts may be very small and detailed. Machinists must be able to detect flaws in these parts.

Machinists must be able to make products that meet high quality standards. Machinists need to cut and shape parts properly. The products must not have any flaws. The products also must meet exact measurements.

Work Styles

Machinists must be able to perform physical work. They may work in cramped workspaces and awkward positions. Machinists often must stand for many hours. Machinists use hoists to lift and move heavy objects. Hoists lift objects so that machinists can work on parts on the objects' undersides. This type of work can be hard on machinists' bodies.

Machinists must practice safety procedures on the job. Machines often operate at high speeds and may produce bits of flying metal. Machinists wear protective safety glasses to shield their eyes from these metal pieces. Machinists also wear earplugs to protect their hearing from the loud noise machines make. Machinists must be careful when handling dangerous cooling and lubricating materials. Lubricating materials keep machines running smoothly. These materials can cause serious injuries if they come into contact with the skin.

Today, computers control many machines. These machines often are safer than machines that are not controlled by computers. But

Skills

Workplace Skills   Yes / No

Resources:
Assign use of time .... ☑ ☐
Assign use of money .... ☐ ☑
Assign use of material and facility resources .... ☑ ☐
Assign use of human resources .... ☐ ☑

Interpersonal Skills:
Take part as a member of a team .... ☑ ☐
Teach others .... ☑ ☐
Serve clients/customers .... ☐ ☑
Show leadership .... ☑ ☐
Work with others to arrive at a decision .... ☑ ☐
Work with a variety of people .... ☑ ☐

Information:
Acquire and judge information .... ☑ ☐
Understand and follow legal requirements .... ☑ ☐
Organize and maintain information .... ☑ ☐
Understand and communicate information .... ☑ ☐
Use computers to process information .... ☑ ☐

Systems:
Identify, understand, and work with systems .... ☑ ☐
Understand environmental, social, political, economic,
    or business systems .... ☑ ☐
Oversee and correct system performance .... ☑ ☐
Improve and create systems .... ☐ ☑

Technology:
Select technology .... ☑ ☐
Apply technology to task .... ☑ ☐
Maintain and troubleshoot technology .... ☑ ☐

Foundation Skills

Basic Skills:
Read .... ☑ ☐
Write .... ☑ ☐
Do arithmetic and math .... ☑ ☐
Speak and listen .... ☑ ☐

Thinking Skills:
Learn .... ☑ ☐
Reason .... ☑ ☐
Think creatively .... ☑ ☐
Make decisions .... ☑ ☐
Solve problems .... ☑ ☐

Personal Qualities:
Take individual responsibility .... ☑ ☐
Have self-esteem and self-management .... ☑ ☐
Be sociable .... ☑ ☐
Be fair, honest, and sincere .... ☑ ☐

machinists still must perform their jobs carefully and follow all safety procedures.

Basic Skills

Machinists need math and science skills. They use math to measure parts and figure sizes and dimensions. Science skills help machinists know the qualities of many types of metals and other materials. These qualities include weight and flexibility. Machinists need to know which qualities are best suited for each part. They also must know how to safely work with the materials.

Machinists must have skills in drafting and blueprint reading. These skills help machinists create instructions for producing parts. These skills also help machinists follow directions.

Machinists should have a basic knowledge of computers and electronics. Today, machines are designed to manufacture parts with fewer human operators. Fewer machinists then are needed to perform each job. But machinists need more technical skills to set up, operate, and maintain computer-controlled machines.

Chapter 4

Preparing for the Career

Machinist training varies among states and provinces. There are no particular requirements to become a machinist. But employers usually prefer workers with a high school diploma and related work experience.

High School

People who want to become machinists can prepare for the career in high school. Students should take machine shop or machine trade courses. These courses teach students about many of the machines and tools that machinists use.

People who want to be machinists should take math classes in high school.

Courses in math and science also are helpful. Math classes help students learn to measure parts and determine part sizes. Science classes help students understand the properties of the materials they work with. Students learn which materials are suitable for constructing certain parts.

Some high schools have technical programs. Students learn career skills in these programs. Students spend about half of the school day studying subjects such as the properties of materials. They also learn about machines and tools. The other half of the day is spent in shop classes. Students receive hands-on training with machines and tools in these classes.

Courses in computers and electronics also are helpful. Employers often prefer to hire machinists with computer and electronics skills.

Some high schools have technical programs for students interested in machining careers.

Post-Secondary Training

After high school, most machinists receive formal training from a vocational or technical college. Students learn the basics of machine work and tool making at these schools. They learn die and mold making. They learn how to operate CNC machinery. Students may study Computer-Aided Drafting (CAD). They learn how to use computers to design products. Students also may study Computer-Aided Manufacturing (CAM). They learn how to use computers to manufacture products.

Most students complete their formal training in one to two years. Students then are ready to work as machinists. New machinists continue to learn through on-the-job training. Experienced machinists provide this training. Machinists usually can work without guidance after six months.

Apprenticeship

Some machinists receive formal training through apprenticeship programs. Apprentices

Most machinists receive formal training from a technical college.

enter a formal agreement with an employer. They agree to work for their employer for a certain amount of time while they learn the trade. Apprentices learn their trade by working with skilled machinists. These machinists instruct the apprentices. Machinist apprentices usually work for their employers for four years. Apprentices also earn salaries.

Machinist apprenticeship programs consist of shop training and related classroom training. Apprentices usually receive about 8,000 hours of on-the-job training. They also receive about 700 hours of classroom instruction. Apprentices learn to operate many machines and tools during on-the-job training.

Classroom instruction includes math, blueprint reading, drafting, and physics. This science is the study of matter and energy. Apprentices also learn to operate and program computer-controlled machines. Apprentices with some formal education usually have a shorter apprenticeship.

Certification

Machinists do not need to be certified in the United States or Canada. But machinists are certified after successfully completing their apprenticeship. In the United States, the Federal Bureau of Apprenticeship and Training grants certification. State apprenticeship agencies also can give certification. Employers know that certified machinists have a full understanding of the profession.

Machinists in Canada who complete apprenticeship programs become certified journeyman machinists. Most employers prefer to hire machinists who are certified journeyman machinists. A journeyman is a person who has completed an apprenticeship. This person should earn the highest minimum wage rate for the job.

Apprentices usually receive about 8,000 hours of on-the-job training.

Chapter 5

The Market

The job market for machinists is strong. Job openings are expected to increase in both the United States and Canada.

Job Outlook

Machinists can find jobs in areas that have a large number of manufacturing companies. Machinists can find jobs in small machining shops or large manufacturing companies.

Many machinists are approaching retirement age. Machinists will be needed to fill these vacancies. Few people are entering machine trade programs to fill these job openings.

Skilled machinists will continue to be in high demand. They will be needed to build machines and tools to produce goods. They

Machinists can find jobs in small machining shops.

Some machinists can advance to computer programming positions.

also will be needed to repair and maintain these machines and tools.

Salary

Machinists' salaries depend on experience and location. In the United States, machinists just entering the field earn $16,120 to $55,000 per year. The average machinist salary is about $38,650 per year.

In Canada, machinists earn about \$20,500 to \$54,800 per year. The average machinist salary is about \$37,700 per year.

Advancement Opportunities

Machinists should continue their education throughout their careers. Advances in technology create machines that are more advanced. Methods of working with metal and other materials also change.

Skilled machinists who continue their education may advance in several ways. Machinists may gain experience by managing other employees. They may move into supervisor or management positions. A shop supervisor can earn as much as \$70,000 per year.

Machinists who specialize have more opportunities to advance. Machining specialties require high degrees of skill and training. Toolmakers and die makers are experts in the machinist field. Other machinists may become programmers. Some machinists become manufacturing engineers. These people are experts at designing and making machines. Some experienced machinists may even open their own machining shops.

Related Careers

People interested in the machining field can work in related careers. People may find careers in metalworking and plastics-working careers. They also may become blacksmiths, gunsmiths, locksmiths, or welders. Blacksmiths make and repair things made of iron. Locksmiths make and repair locks and keys. Welders make and repair things made of metal or plastic.

Machines will continue to play an important part in people's lives. Machines help produce many of the products people use every day. Machinists will be needed to operate and maintain these machines.

People interested in the machining field may find careers in welding.